Bright
Summaries.com

In the Shadow of the Flowering Maidens

BY MARCEL PROUST

BOOK ANALYSIS

Written by Irène Lazzari
Translated by Oliver Brown

In the Shadow of the Flowering Maidens

BY MARCEL PROUST

MARCEL PROUST

FRENCH WRITER

- **Born in 1871 in Paris**

- **Died 1922 in Paris**

- **Some of his works:**

  - *Swann's Way* (1913), novel

  - *Albertine disparue* (1925), novel

  - *Le temps retrouvé* (1927), novel

Born into a wealthy and cultured family, Marcel Proust attended aristocratic salons from an early age, where he met artists and writers. From childhood, his health was particularly fragile and he suffered from serious respiratory problems throughout his life. Taking advantage of his family fortune, he devoted all his time to writing and in 1907 began writing his work *In Search of Lost Time*. This vast novelistic fresco consists of seven volumes, which were published between 1913 and 1927, the last four being published posthumously. Marcel Proust's novelistic work is gigantic; with more than two hundred characters, it offers a reflection on time, emotional memory, the functions of art, and also a meditation on human feelings such as love, jealousy, homosexuality and the feeling of failure. For all these reasons, Marcel Proust has established himself as one of the greatest writers of the twentieth century and is considered throughout the world to be the most representative of French literature. Indeed, more theoretical works have been written about him than about any other French writer, so resounding was his legacy.

IN THE SHADOW OF THE FLOWERING MAIDENS

FIRST LOVE AND FIRST LITERARY RECOGNITION

- **Genre:** novel

- **Reference edition**: À l'ombre des jeunes filles en fleurs, Paris, Le Livre de Poche, 1992, 667 p.

- **1st edition:** 1919

- **Themes:** aristocracy, society, love, jealousy, art, writing, memories, illness

À l'ombre des jeunes filles en fleurs is the second volume of the novel *À la recherche du temps perdu*, which consists of seven volumes and three thousand pages. Published in 1919, it won the Goncourt Prize the same year, which marked the beginning of a prestigious recognition that would continue to grow over time. The novel faithfully continues the story of the first volume, *Du côté de chez Swann*, and thus includes the same characters while adding new ones.

The question of autobiography has often been discussed, as the narrator has certain characteristics similar to those of Marcel Proust. Indeed, the narrative takes place from the internal point of view, i.e. with the personal pronoun 'I', and the narrator, besides being called Marcel, is also a writer in poor health, from a wealthy family and frequenting the aristocratic salons of the time. However, Proust always made it clear that the writer and the man were two different entities and that it would be simplistic to see any autobiographical intention in his work. *In the Shadow of Young Girls in Bloom* continues to be read all over the world a century later thanks to dozens of translations and remains one of the great classics of French literature.

SUMMARY

The novel is divided into two parts. The first, 'Around Madame Swann', relates the narrator's relationships with figures from Parisian society and, in particular, with Gilberte Swann, for whom he has a love that gradually deteriorates. In the second, 'Nom de pays: Le pays', he settles in Balbec and experiences a very solitary existence, until he meets and befriends a number of young girls. Among them, one in particular, named Albertine, interests him; he falls in love with her.

AROUND MME SWANN

The narrator's parents receive a visit from Monsieur de Norpois. Marcel is about fifteen years old at the time, but he listens attentively to the visitor talk about Monsieur and Madame Swann, friends from whom his parents have grown distant over the years. Secretly in love with their daughter, Gilberte, Marcel suggests to Monsieur de Norpois that he would like to be received at the Swanns' house, but the latter seems unresponsive. Together they have a long conversation about Bergotte, a well-known writer whom Marcel greatly admires, although Monsieur de Norpois does not share this admiration. This is followed by a discussion about Marcel's future, as his parents predict a career in the diplomatic service, whereas the young man has a gift for writing and is more interested in a literary future. However, Marcel is plagued by doubts as his motivation fluctuates, but feels reassured that a large family inheritance, from his aunt Léonie, will always keep him out of poverty.

During his walks along the Champs-Élysées, Marcel flirts with Gilberte Swann, constantly seeking contact with the body of this young woman whom he likes so much and who also seems to like him. The narrator experiences the first symptoms of asthma, a disease that will bother him for the rest of his life, and seeks treatment from Dr. Cottard, a man of little education but very well known in his field, who offers Marcel a treatment that is unfortunately not very effective.

Marcel is delighted to be invited by Gilberte, more and more frequently, to the home of her parents, the Swanns, whose reputation is tarnished by their Republican affiliations. At their home he meets Bergotte, the eminent writer he admires so much, but he is unpleasantly surprised by his appearance, his bearing and his strange speech. Bergotte noticed Marcel's sharp mind and potential and was particularly attentive to the young man, while his parents looked on admiringly. The visits became more and more frequent.

Together with his friend, Albert Bloch, a young man who displeases Marcel's family, they go to a very poor brothel where the narrator meets Rachel, one of the boarders. Gilberte is increasingly annoyed by the frequency of Marcel's visits to her home and wishes to end the relationship by limiting it to mere correspondence, which causes Marcel great pain. When he notices that Gilberte is in the company of a young man, he becomes very jealous and goes to console himself with some girls of joy.

COUNTRY NAME: THE COUNTRY

Two years have passed between the two parts of the story and Marcel has gone to Balbec with his grandmother, whom he loves dearly, to treat his asthma. They are staying at the Grand-Hotel in Balbec, in a room that is unfamiliar to him and where he struggles to find his bearings, but he is seduced by the proximity of the ocean and the conviviality of the meals taken by the water's edge on the veranda. The young man's shyness prevents him from making friends with the young people he would like to meet. He meets Madame de Villeparisis, the mistress of Monsieur de Norpois, a very liberal and broad-minded woman who seduces him. He then befriends his nephew, Robert de Saint-Loup, but when Albert Bloch joins Marcel in Balbec, the latter tries to divide them by saying bad things about each of them.

Since his arrival, Marcel has noticed a group of young girls and feels particularly attracted to one of them because of her beauty. He leads a very disorganised life, going to bed early in the morning, but justifies his laziness by his poor health. He meets Elstir, a famous painter, through whom he meets Albertine, the girl he has been observing for a long time, as well as Andrée and Gisèle, his friends. Marcel spends a lot of time with this group of girls, to the point of abandoning his grandmother. Together they go to the beach and the hotel casino to have a good time; Marcel is perfectly happy.

During a tea party with friends, Albertine slips him a small note with the message "I like you". Later, when the young girl has to spend a night at the Grand Hotel, she invites Marcel to come and visit her in her room. The young man is euphoric at this proposal and, when the time comes, while she is lying on the bed, he tries to kiss her, but is brutally refused. From then on, he turns away from her for a while and turns his attention to Andrée, hoping to arouse Albertine's jealousy.

The season ends, the rooms of the Grand Hotel empty one by one, the casino closes and the weather turns rainy. The girls, Albertine first, leave Balbec, leaving Marcel more and more alone, until he decides to return to Paris. All his efforts to get closer to her were to no avail and Marcel is left with a bitter taste.

CHARACTER STUDY

MARCEL, A NARRATOR WHO LONGS FOR ART AND LOVE

À l'ombre des jeunes filles en fleurs is a narrative written in the first person: it is therefore through this "I" that the emotions, feelings and descriptions are experienced and recounted. The narrator, the hero of the novel, is called Marcel and his age, in this volume, is at the end of adolescence. His entry into the adult world is marked by specific ambitions, as he aspires to become an artist, and more specifically a writer. However, due to the preoccupations of his adolescence, he is strongly troubled by the search for love and his attraction to young girls occupies much of his thoughts.

Very curious by nature, Marcel likes to listen to the conversations of the people around him in order to learn about the functioning of life in society. He is also very ambitious and wants to be integrated into the social spheres that revolve around his parents, and in particular the Swann family, firstly because he is very attracted to Gilberte, Monsieur Swann's daughter, and secondly because he has great admiration for her father, Charles Swann. The latter, a wealthy dandy, elegant, discreet and a connoisseur of the arts, was a close associate of the Parisian aristocracy. From then on, Marcel took a great interest in this character, and then in the artists whom the latter received at his home, such as the writer Bergotte.

Marcel is also a young man who is very attached to his childhood and youthful memories and his imagination is extremely fertile, especially when he is in love. His sensitivity and shyness sometimes prevent him from finding his place among the people he meets, especially with young people his own age. His asthmatic illness hinders his daily life and he sometimes takes refuge behind it to legitimise his laziness. On the other hand, his family fortune protects him from precariousness and he wishes to devote his life to writing.

From a sentimental point of view, Marcel is a very jealous character who cannot stand competition and has difficulty trusting women. He doubts the sincerity of women, especially Albertine, and subjects her to an interrogation to find out how she spends her time, both past and present. He spies on her every move and showers her with gifts, hoping to buy her docility.

CHARLES SWANN

The character of Charles Swann is very present in the previous volume (*Du côté de chez Swann*) and remains omnipresent in the whole cycle, mainly in *À l'ombre des jeunes filles en fleurs*. A wealthy dandy, he owns a castle near Combray and keeps close company with the Parisian aristocracy as well as with the artists and writers of the time. He is not known to have any professional activity, except for writing a biography of a Flemish painter, which will remain unfinished. Very charming by nature, he played the role of a wealthy dandy, which Marcel greatly enjoyed. After collecting a number of female conquests, he married Odette de Crécy, a somewhat opportunistic socialite. Their marriage was the cause of a social decline, as it was very badly perceived by the petty bourgeoisie and Marcel's parents.

Aware of his wife's rejection, he shuns her company when he goes to social dinners or social gatherings. Although he was very discreet in Combray, in Paris he led a social life where he rubbed shoulders with the greatest celebrities.

Proust was inspired by the real-life character Charles Hass, a contemporary of his who frequented the literary salons. Also a wealthy Jew, the young man lived in a worldly way without exercising any profession.

GILBERTE, A CRUEL FIRST LOVE

Gilberte is the daughter of Charles Swann and Odette de Crécy. After hearing about her for a long time, Marcel dreams of meeting her. He met her for the first time during a walk on the Champs-Élysées and this meeting remains engraved in his memory.

Gilberte is a teenager who is aware of her beauty and its effect on Marcel. From then on, she abuses her charms somewhat to play with his feelings, notably by pushing him away and then making him come back to her for a snack at the family home. She soon tires of his frequent visits and makes him feel that his presence is no longer desirable. Moreover, she is particularly cruel to the narrator by making false confidences: while Marcel rightly thinks that he is very much appreciated by the girl's parents, she replies that her parents do not appreciate him at all and that they would even be delighted to know that their daughter has stopped seeing him.

She is quite charismatic by nature and likes to please men, and Marcel learns much later, via Gilberte's maid, that she was seeing another man very frequently during her relationship with the narrator. Gilberte behaves like a spoiled child with Marcel and their relationship deteriorates to the point where it is limited to a few letters. Marcel hopes that Gilberte will finally beg him to return, but she never does. To add insult to injury, when she invites Marcel to her house for the last time, loaded with gifts in preparation for a reconciliation, Gilberte is on the arm of another young man near the meeting point.

In *À la recherche du temps perdu*, the character of Gilberte embodies the first love that young Marcel is confronted with, with all its passion, but also with its cruelty. Indeed, the experience with Gilberte will be a source of great suffering.

ALBERTINE, A BEAUTIFUL ENIGMA

Albertine Simonet is a young girl who belongs to the bourgeoisie. Marcel meets her for the first time in Balbec with his gang, riding a bicycle. She is an important character, as she will reappear in all the other volumes of *À la recherche du temps perdu*. The narrator describes her at length after having observed her regularly from his hotel room. Her physical appearance is enigmatic, as this descriptive extract shows:

> *But more often than not she was more coloured, and then more animated; sometimes only the tip of her nose was pink, in her white face, as fine as that of a sly little cat with which one would have liked to play; sometimes her cheeks were so smooth that one's gaze glided as if over a miniature's on their pink enamel, which was made to appear even more delicate, more interior, by the half-open and superimposed lid of her black hair; sometimes the complexion of her cheeks reached the purplish pink of cyclamen, and sometimes even when she was congested or feverish, and then gave the idea of a sickly complexion which reduced my desire to something more sensual and made her look express something more perverse and unhealthy, the dark purple of certain roses, of an almost black red; and each of these Albertines was different, as each of the dancer's appearances is different, whose colours, form and character are transmuted by the innumerable games of a luminous projector. (pp. 586-587)*

Albertine is very intelligent and has refined taste in painting and dress. However, the narrator finds her ill-mannered and impertinent, and does not appreciate her slang language. Indeed, on the second date, he is taken aback by a rude tone of voice that he was not familiar with. He is also very unsettled by the possibility that she is homosexual. At the casino, for example, Albertine engages in a rather lascivious dance with her friend Andrée. Her relationships with her gang of friends are seen as ambiguous and Marcel is increasingly doubtful about her morality and the deceptions she is capable of. In addition, Albertine sometimes makes anti-Semitic remarks, notably when she says she is disgusted with Marcel's friend Bloch because of his Jewish background, and then with his sisters.

Albertine shares a character trait with Gilberte, since she too is rather confusing when it comes to seduction: when she invites Marcel to join her in her room and he tries to kiss her, she violently refuses. She too is aware of the desire she is capable of arousing in a man and plays on it.

BERGOTTE, WITHOUT LOOKING LIKE IT

Bergotte is a famous writer whom Marcel meets for the first time at the Swanns' house. A gentle man of great kindness, he makes a dedication to the young man who admires him despite the jealousy he feels when he learns that Bergotte and Gilberte often visit old monuments together.

Bergotte is not at all appreciated by Monsieur de Norpois; the latter is constantly criticising him, questioning his literary qualities and his intelligence, because, according to him, his mind is confused, he is sometimes vulgar and his books are boring. Influenced by Monsieur de Norpois, Marcel's father is also very harsh towards him, but suddenly softens when Begrotte praises Marcel for his intelligence.

Marcel is very surprised by his physical appearance, which is far from what he had imagined: he is short, stocky, short-sighted, his nose is red and he has a black goatee. He is also surprised by his voice, which seems to be totally different from the way he writes. Marcel says of him: "Bergotte did not look like a Bergotte" (p.167), thus demonstrating the deconstruction of the fantasy representation he had of this admirable writer.

Although he is not a prominent character in the novel, he is nonetheless important, since it is under his encouragement that Marcel decides to become a writer as well, abandoning his parents' dream of a diplomatic career. Bergotte returns in the second part of the novel: he visits Marcel, his mother and his grandmother at the Grand-Hôtel in Balbec.

ELSTIR, IMPRESSIONIST PAINTER

Elstir was a renowned painter who became a friend of Charles Swann. Marcel met him for the first time in Balbec and was so impressed by his talent that he wrote a letter to him at a dinner party, enthusiastically expressing his admiration and asking permission to pay his respects.

Elstir embodied talent and excitement: an anecdote reveals that he took a model to the seaside in the middle of the night to pose nude in the moonlight. Marcel was extremely happy and touched by Elstir's generosity when he invited him to visit his studio. There, Marcel made a disconcerting discovery when he noticed that one of his old paintings depicted Odette de Crécy, Charles Swann's future wife.

It is Elstir who, at Marcel's request, introduces the narrator to Albertine.

KEYS TO READING

PROUST AND BIOGRAPHY

In Search of Lost Time is a novelistic cycle that represents a temporal continuum, from childhood memories in Combray to adulthood and life in Paris, and involves the interaction of nearly three thousand characters. Despite the strong similarities that the narrator shares with the author, Proust has always denied any autobiographical ambition. However, he himself did not really know what term could best describe his work, and his correspondence of the time, dated 1909 – a year after the writing of the first volume began – reveals an ambiguity, as he refers to "a whole long book", "not a novel", but nevertheless "a novel", or "an important work (let us say a novel, because it is a kind of novel)".

It is difficult to ignore the fundamental differences between the Marcel we read and the Marcel who writes: the former is neither Jewish nor homosexual. Moreover, in *À l'ombre des jeunes filles en fleurs*, Balbec is an imaginary town. Indeed, it is described as a seaside resort in Normandy, and Marcel Proust's visits to Cabourd were a strong inspiration for the creation of this novelistic town.

Benoit de Sainte-Beuve, a famous critic of the mid-nineteenth century, explained that a writer's work echoed his or her life and that, in order to understand it, it was necessary to take an interest in the author and his or her life. This method of approaching texts was therefore based on the search for poetic intention - also known as intentionism - and a biographical reading. However, in his famous essay *Contre Sainte-Beuve*, Marcel Proust retorts:

> *Sainte-Beuve's work is not a profound work [...] this method ignores what a somewhat profound relationship with ourselves teaches us: that a book is the product of another self than the one we manifest in our habits, in society, in our vices. [...] At no time does Sainte-Beuve seem to have understood what is special about inspiration and literary work, and what differentiates it entirely from the occupations of other men and the other occupations of the writer.*

 DID YOU KNOW THAT?

When Marcel Proust presented his first volume - *Du côté de chez Swann* - his manuscript was rejected by all the Parisian publishers! He then decided to publish his 712 pages with Grasset on a self-publishing basis - that is, by financing the publication himself.

THE PORTRAIT OF THE YOUNG GIRLS IN BLOOM

Proust is a writer who places great importance on the descriptive in his work. Close to the painters of his time - notably Pablo Picasso -, an art lover and regular visitor to the Parisian salons, he punctuated his novels with numerous moments of contemplation or references to real or fictional works of art. The character of Elstir, in *À l'ombre des jeunes filles en fleurs*, is inspired by Impressionist painters such as Claude Monet, Édouard

Manet and Auguste Renoir. Proust himself, when drawing a portrait of a character, is careful to give a very complete description, both of a face and of a body.

Changing portraits

The descriptions give way to portraits that can be read and that reveal, in the manner of a painter, the physical characteristics of the character, sometimes using terms borrowed from the world of painting. This is the case, for example, with the portrait of Rachel, the *fille de joie* he meets in a brothel, whose black hair is "irregular as if it had been indicated by crosshatching in a wash, in Indian ink". When Marcel describes Albertine as she stands by the sea, he compares her profile to those of the women of Paul Veronese, a sixteenth-century Italian painter. As for Gilberte, he likens her to Melusine, a fairy-like character from a medieval legend often depicted in pictorial and sculptural art – among others by Jean d'Arras, Julius Hübner, and Ludwig Michael von Schwanthaler. If Proust chooses to use the image of Melusine, it is not only to evoke this motif superficially: Melusine is a serpent woman linked to the myth of the Original Sin as presented in the Bible, and we can therefore guess a form of guilt associated with sexuality.

But this tendency to mix literature with painting does not only concern the characters. Indeed, at many points, the narrator compares places he discovers to scenes in paintings. This is the case when Marcel is invited to eat at the Swanns' house and Gilberte takes him into the dining room: "And she took us into the dining room, dark as the interior of an Asian Temple painted by Rembrandt".

From then on, the scenes in which a new character appears are an opportunity for the narrator to draw up a portrait. In this sense, Marcel is an aesthete who seeks beauty in everyday life and *À l'ombre des jeunes filles en fleurs* is particularly representative of this curiosity and attraction for the female gender, since the story is set in his teenage years, i.e. at a time when the young man is beginning to feel desire and fascination for the other sex.

Moreover, Marcel evokes these moments when he tries to capture the beauty of the loved one and draws a parallel between the person observed and the person remembered:

> *"The searching, anxious, demanding way in which we look at the person we love, our expectation of the word that will give us or take away the hope of a rendezvous for the next day, and, until that word is spoken, our alternative, if not simultaneous, imagination of joy and despair, all this makes our attention in front of the beloved too tremulous to obtain a clear-cut image of him. Perhaps also this activity of all the senses at once, and which tries to know with the eyes alone what is beyond them, is too indulgent to the thousand forms, to all the flavours, to the movements of the living person that usually, when we do not love, we immobilise." p.103)*

Finally, Marcel is in a state of exaltation when he is with Albertine by a fire and her round face seems so moving to him that he compares it to the figures painted by Michelangelo, carried away by a 'motionless and dizzying whirlwind'.

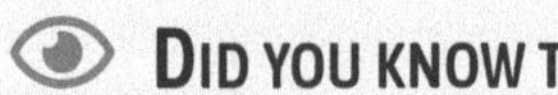

DID YOU KNOW THAT?

Marcel Proust is known as the author of very long, elaborate sentences, and there is even an adjective derived from his name to describe his long-winded writing. Indeed, a complicated sentence with many juxtapositions can be described as 'Proustian'. This is not surprising when you know that in *Sodom and Gomorrah,* the fourth part of *La Recherche*, the longest sentence contains 856 words!

SATIRE OF THE BOURGEOISIE AND THE ARISTOCRACY

The novel is set in the bourgeois society of the early twentieth century, and many of the characters are from the aristocracy. Marcel Proust himself comes from a wealthy family, highly educated and well integrated into the social salons; however, he does not fail to use irony to describe this society and goes so far as to satirize, i.e. to mock, the hypocrisy reigning in this societal sphere.

A conditioned admiration

The narrator begins gently with an anecdote about his parents who, at first reluctant to have their son associate with the writer Bergotte, whom they consider mediocre, then suddenly show admiration for him when he praises Marcel's intelligence. This sudden change of heart about the writer is based on a compliment to their offspring, and as image-conscious parents, they want to be surrounded by positive people.

What will people say?

When Monsieur Swann marries Odette de Crécy, the petty bourgeoisie is very sceptical about this woman who is only half a socialite. Because of this marriage, Marcel's parents distance themselves from Monsieur Swann. He himself is aware of his wife's social decline and goes alone to the receptions to which he is invited so as not to face the mockery of others.

Titles of nobility

Proust uses a comic device to show the absurdity of titles of nobility. When the narrator is walking along the Champs-Élysées with Françoise, his Aunt Léonie's cook, and they go to the toilet, an old lady 'with plastered cheeks and a red wig' starts talking to him. Françoise then reveals that this "madame pipi" is in fact a marquise who belongs to the Saint-Ferréol family. The comedy of the situation results from the glaring discrepancy between the old lady's status and her offbeat appearance and work. Moreover, Proust uses inverted commas when referring to this marquise in order to highlight the deception.

When the narrator mentions a princess of the blood who regularly dines at Madame de Guermantes', he regrets that she is invited only because of her title and not because of her spirit. Marcel even adds: 'But with the naivety of people of the world, as soon as she was received, we tried to find her agreeable, for want of being able to say to ourselves that it was because we had found her agreeable that she was received' (p.127). Thus Proust denounces the hollow archaism of worldly people to surround themselves with characters for their title alone.

In Balbec, Marcel witnesses the arrival of the Princess of Luxembourg, who arrives in a carriage and offers him her hand. She fills the young man's pockets with candy canes and small tied packages. Despite his young age, Marcel notices the condescension of the princess, who goes for a walk while someone shelters him under an umbrella.

MISUNDERSTANDING OF LOVE AND EXCESSIVE JEALOUSY

Marcel is thus an adolescent preoccupied with sentimental issues and carnal desires. When Monsieur de Norpois mentions the Swann family at the beginning of the novel, Marcel remembers the young Gilberte and, in the process of remembering, thinks of her in a very specific way. When he then sees her on the Champs-Élysées, he has to confront the idealised representation of his fantasies with the young woman he is looking at and is disappointed, as if the imagination had fed his desire for her too much and objective reality caught up with him. However, he feels a great deal of desire for Gilberte and as they play together he cannot help but seek contact with her body. The hands are already a little touchy and his desire intensifies as their bodies touch.

A difficult quest

With Gilberte, the frustration of not meeting her more quickly gives rise to numerous fantasies, while with Albertine, the fact that he watches her for days on end on the beach helps to make her a quest that must be appropriated. There is no such thing as easy love. So when Marcel goes to a brothel and meets one of the residents, Rachel, he feels no pleasure in conquering this woman who has already been offered. The strength of love is necessarily the result of the difficulty he has in obtaining what he wants.

His rapprochement with Gilberte makes him happy as it foreshadows a future love affair, but when he senses that she is drifting away, he is even more determined to win her over. When, at Gilberte's insistence, their relationship is limited to letters, Marcel shows his pride by hoping that she will be the one to beg him to return. This desire to be with her becomes a source of suffering.

With Albertine, the approach is similar as the young woman seems to be playing cat and mouse with Marcel, which does not fail to irritate him. He is even more disappointed when he is invited to join her in her room and she, despite what the situation suggests, refuses to accept his kisses.

An all-consuming jealousy

Whether with Gilberte or Albertine, Marcel's all-consuming jealousy is detrimental to his well-being and to the budding complicity he shares with these young women. He constantly questions Gilberte about her appointments, tries to find out her schedule and is suspicious of her. When he sees her with another young man, he goes to a brothel to try to forget her.

With Albertine, the narrator is plagued by questions about her morality, suspecting her of having sexual relations with the friends of his gang. His jealousy and possessiveness towards Gilberte are nevertheless given a tangible foundation when he learns, much later, that she was seeing another man more often than he was. Once again, Marcel shows pride and manipulation with Albertine, for when she refuses him, he suddenly prefers his friend Andrée, and hopes that this radical change will arouse regrets in her.

AVENUES FOR REFLECTION

A FEW QUESTIONS FOR FURTHER REFLECTION...

* Who recognises Marcel in one of the paintings in Elstir's studio? What does this mean?

* Under what circumstances does Marcel meet Rachel?

* Why does Marcel laugh at his grandmother when she poses for a photograph and what are her reasons for wanting to be immortalised in this way?

* Are the two parts of the novel dependent on each other?

* How does Proust deal with the theme of homosexuality?

* How do the narrator's pride and jealousy manifest themselves? What are the consequences?

* How would you describe Marcel Proust's style?

* Where is Balbec and what is special about the Grand Hotel where he lives?

* Why does Albertine decide to take a room at the Grand Hotel?

* What similarities and differences do the narrator and the writer share?

- Why does Marcel want to meet Bergotte?

- Marcel has a great admiration for Monsieur Swann, why?

- How does Marcel feel about Odette de Crécy?

TO GO FURTHER

REFERENCE EDITION

PROUST M., À l'ombre des jeunes filles en fleurs, Paris, Le Livre de Poche, 1992, 667 p.

BENCHMARK STUDIES

Correspondance de Marcel Proust, établie, annotée et préfacée par Philip Kolb, Paris, Plon, 21 vols. 1970-1993; t. VIII, p. 250

ERMAN M., Le Bottin des lieux proustiens, La Table ronde, 2011

HENRY A., La Tentation de Proust, Paris, PUF, 2000

MIGUER-OLLAGNIER M., La Mythologie de Marcel Proust, Paris, Les Belles Lettres, coll. « Annales littéraires de l'Université de Besançon », 1982, 425 p.

PRIEUR J., Marcel avant Proust, followed by Proust, Le Mensuel retrouvé, éditions des Busclats, 2012

TAMRAZ N., Proust Portrait Peinture, Paris, Orizons, coll. Universités/Domaine littéraire, 2010

VAGO D., Proust en couleur, « Recherches proustiennes » collection, Honoré Champion, 2012

VULTUR, I., La réception de la Recherche: une question de genre? at https://www.cairn.info/revue-poetique-2005-2-page-239.htm [accessed 18 October 2018]

ZAGDANSKY S., Le Sexe de Proust, Gallimard, 1994

Your opinion is important to us!
Leave a comment on the website of your online bookshop
and share your favourites on social networks!

Ebook EAN: 9782808686716
Paperback EAN: 9782808698115
Legal Deposit: D/2023/12603/1091

Cover: © Primento
Digital conception by Primento, the digital partner of publishers.